AF221153

Ariel

Love Wild

Bibliografische Information der Deutschen Nationalbibliothek:

Die Deutsche Nationalbibliothek verzeichnet diese Publikation in der Deutschen Nationalbibliografie; detaillierte bibliografische Daten sind im Internet über http://dnb.dnb.de abrufbar.

Herstellung und Verlag: BoD –
Books on Demand, Norderstedt

ISBN: 978-3-7526-5794-4

Months had passed since Ariel had seen her friend, Gabriel. There was a missing person report filed, but nothing had turned up yet. She, along with various family members and friends of his, searched every night for weeks. They would even go miles out near state borders to find him. The news was devastating. Gabriel was a top student in his college and was near graduation for electrical engineering. There was just too much promise for a young man like him to be so easily swept away and lost in the world. By now, the worst was thought since there had been no findings or clues at all. Officially, the case was ruled as a murder once nothing turned up to prove he was otherwise alive. The authorities would still work to find Gabriel, but now that were searching for a body and not a person.

Ariel didn't take the news very well. She spent most of her time in her apartment and didn't go out much at all. She had always been a vibrant and cheerful person, especially when around Gabriel. Now, she always had her mid-back length dark red hair up in a messy bun or ponytail and she'd just wear some old shirts and a t-shirt to go out. She didn't have the energy to do much else past getting dressed and decent for public interactions. What's worse is that she had lost a few pounds as well due to her lack of eating caused by her depression and despair. Truth be told, Gabriel was more than a friend to her. Whether he realized it or not, Ariel had feelings for him that went beyond friendship. She was never brave enough to express these feelings, though. The possibility of straining their relationship or losing a friend made her too nervous to do anything about it. After his disappearance, she regretted her inaction. She could have told him and maybe they'd be together now. Maybe they would have been together the night he disappeared and she could have stopped it.

Tonight, something was itching at her. She felt the need to go outside and get some fresh air which is a feeling she hadn't had in a long while. She managed to get herself dressed in a pair of jeans and a tank top, a step up from what she usually wore as of late. She let her hair down and put a brush through it to get her red, wavy locks a bit more tame after being up in buns for so long. After looking herself over in the mirror and putting on her shoes, she was out the door and already knew where she was heading. There was a small park not too far from her apartment. Not many people went there, especially not at night. It held a few benches and was mostly surrounded by trees, and there was no play equipment set up. She used to come here a lot with Gabriel to hang out and talk. Those were the times where she really wanted to tell him how she felt, but never developed the courage to do so. She wasn't sure why she was compelled to go there, but she had arrived and wandered over to the small bench the pair would sit at when they came. She hesitantly sat down as if she was about to plop down on something sharp. A small pain went through her, but it wasn't anything that was on the bench. It was as if a pang went through her heart now that she was taking it all in and admitting to herself that her best friend was really... gone. She'd never given herself time to process his likely death, and now that she was out here in the park that held so many memories, it all came crashing down on her.

Ariel started crying, sobbing really. She had her face in her hands and they quickly became damp with her tears. Her anguish was unhindered and had quite a bit of volume to it as all of her despair poured out of her, all of it that had been bottled up inside. Her body shook and her breathing was uneven and labored as she took in shaky breaths and let them out in her shaky sobs. She wasn't paying attention to anything else around her at all. As far as she was concerned, she was in her own world of turmoil. No one was at the small park so late at night, anyway. Even if someone was around, she wasn't sure if she'd care or if she'd be embarrassed at all. It was due to her inattention that when she felt a touch to her shoulder, she cried out sharply in sudden fright.

Her shriek was cut short as a hand went around her mouth to silence her. Another arm went around her front and restrained her arms. Now she was absolutely terrified and the strength of whoever restrained her was even more frightening. She couldn't even move as she writhed and struggled, her whimpers and protests muffled against the hand at her mouth.

"Ariel, please." Pleaded a male voice behind her. "I need you to be quiet."

She froze and her eyes widened. That voice. It was Gabriel's. At least, it sounded like him... a lot. He also knew her name, and the way he held onto her was fairly gentle even if applying a surprising amount of strength. Then again, with all the trauma she'd been through, maybe she was hallucinating the sound of his voice or something. Still, she stopped struggling and tried to relax even as she panted heavily, making herself light-headed.

"It's me, Ariel. Gabriel." He said finally. "Just please... don't scream or anything." That was a strange request coming from her missing friend.

The young woman nodded and relaxed her arms. She had no idea what was going on, but if it was really Gabriel, she'd start crying again!

He released her and jumped over the bend to stand in front of her. That was... quite a feat. It only took one glance to know it was him. He was tall, at least 6'2", short dark brown hair that was just long enough to need a comb, striking green eyes, lightly tanned skin, and the most warming smile. He looked down at her, clearly nervous but smiling. "Hey, Ariel." He spoke softly.

Her eyes were wide as she stared up at him in shock, relief, joy. After a few moments, she shot up and wrapped her arms around. "Gabriel?! Oh my God! How? Where? I..." She stammered out, her breathing still erratic.

He held her by her arms and made her look up into his eyes. "Calm down. You're gonna make yourself pass out." Gabriel was clearly concerned but still had that same soft expression on his face.

She nodded quickly, trying to calm herself and gain control of her breathing. "I just... can't believe it. Do your parents know? Have you seen them? W-we haeve to go-!"

He shook his head and leaned down to be face to face with her. "Only you. And I shouldn't even be here." He was strangely serious and his voice sounded grave.

"What?" Ariel's brow furrowed. She didn't understand.

"It's... hard to explain, Ariel. I've been away for months. But I came back now... I just had to see you. I didn't want you to think I was dead." His voice was earnest and there was clearly something he wasn't saying that he was trying to skip around.

"I don't understand. Why did you leave like that?" She was hurt and on the brink of tears again.

"I didn't leave. I was taken." He wasn't joking. "You would never believe." He frowned and let go of her. "I have to go. I shouldn't be here."

He was being so vague, so odd. This wasn't like him at all. "No, wait." She urged him and took his arm in her grasp. "Please just tell me what's going on. I've been so... I... for months..." She stammered out.

Gabriel took a close look at her and appeared devastated. "You look awful." Well, that sure was blunt. "Have you been eating well?" He reached out and held one of her cheeks, gently moving her head around to get a good look at her. "You're smaller and you look so... tired."

Now she felt ashamed. She couldn't just go off and blame him for disrupting her life. She chose everything she did because of her depression. Still, he didn't answer her directly.

"Gabriel, I need to know. Please just tell me." She said slowly and softly, trying to keep her composure.

He closed his eyes and sighed out. "Fine." He sat her down with him on the bench and placed a hand on her knee. "Just listen, okay?" He paused for an answer, satisfied with a nod she gave him. "I was walking home and some guy just grabbed me." He shifted in his seat. "It was at night in that back way I take, ya know? Next thing I know, the dude was biting me. I thought it was some homeless person or something, some crazy person. I passed out. Next thing I know, I was in a room. Like, a really nice room. I felt different. I felt better. But every sound and smell was overwhelming. The same man was in the room with me. He told me he "turned me" to be his "progeny"." He furrowed his brow and shook his head. Why was he telling her all of this? "Ariel, uh... I don't know how else to say this."

Her eyes were wide as she listened. This was insane. What was he even talking about? Ariel leaned in closer to him and placed a hand on his thigh to try and calm him even though she was panicking inside herself. "Just tell me." She urged him.

"Fuck." He groaned. "It's crazy. I'm a vampire." He grimaced as he awaited her reaction.

For the moment, she just stared at him. She blinked a few times and tilted her head. "Huh?"

He wasn't surprised by the reaction. There was one simple way to convince her, but she would scream and probably try to run which would end poorly for him more than likely. "Shit." He cursed again. "Sorry." He apologized and it quickly became clear as to why. He took her by her shoulders and pushed her onto the ground so that he was straddling her hips and had her arms restrained above her head with one strong hand while his other hand covered her mouth. His eyes turned a crimson red and as he neared her, it was clear he had fangs where his canines should be. "Do you get it now?"

There was no way this was a joke or some trick. His strength was incredible and his eyes, his teeth... "Mmf..." She huffed against his muffled hand. The red headed girl wasn't even struggling.

After a moment, Gabriel hesitantly release her arms and her mouth as he looked down at her. He remained atop her, just in case.

"You're a vampire." Ariel stated, almost in question. "You're... but that's..." She shook her head and sat up a little with her elbows holding herself up. Her head was swimming but she fought to keep conscious.

If she fainted now, she might not ever see Gabriel again!

"Yeah." He nodded. "Crazy. Shitty." He said bitterly. Finally, he scooted off of her and sat by her side, helping her up. "Here."

Ariel took his hand and sat up next to him. "I feel sick." She groaned.

"I figured you'd say something like that. I'm a monster from a storybook," He sighed out and started to get up to leave. "I'll... leave you alone, Ariel. I just wanted you to know-"

He was interrupted as she stood up and took his hand. "Please don't leave." She pleaded. "It's... a lot to process. I feel like I'm gonna throw up." She blushed sheepishly. Not something she wanted to admit really. "But it's not because of you. It's just... every-thing."

He looked at her in surprise. Then he frowned and squeezed her hand. "I have to go, Ariel. Being here puts you in danger. If he knew... he probably knows." He pursed his lips and growled lowly, mad about something. "I... I'll try to come back. Please, keep this to yourself."

She nodded slowly and bit her bottom lip. She had so many questions, but she felt like if she heard too much more she really would faint. "Yeah. I promise. Just come see me again. Please."

Gabriel leaned in and kissed her cheek. "I'll try." His words seemed honest, but he was also unsure. He wanted to see her again, deeply. But it was as if it wasn't in his control to do so. "Live better, Ariel." He managed a smile and then turned and ran, faster than any person Ariel had ever seen.

She fell back against the bench and just sat there like a lump. "Holy crap."

Over the next week, Ariel did find herself in better spirits. Keeping her friend's secret did prove to be difficult at times. Especially when she was around their mutual friends. Actually, it was easy to keep the vampire bit secret, but he wasn't missing anymore. He wasn't dead... not in the most literal sense, anyway.

Even though she was still distracted, it was in a much different way. She acted herself around her friends and was more lively. They were all just relieved that their friend wasn't wallowing in depression anymore. Her incredibly chipper behavior was new, though. She dressed nicely and always looked well kept with her deep red hair shining and flowing freely around her shoulders and down to her back. She wore a long sleeved flowing purple shirt that was made of thin fabric to make it airy and a pair of shorts that showed off her legs.

"Hey, Ariel." One of her friends spoke directly to her. She was with a group of four others at a local cafe sitting at their usual table.

Ariel looked up with a smile, obviously off in her own world moments before. "Huh, yeah?"

"So, we were thinkin' of holding our own memorial for Gabriel." The male spoke carefully and softly, unsure of how stable his friend was at this point. She was the closest to Gabriel out of all of them and she had taken the loss hard before. He only brought it up because she seemed to be doing better now.

"Really?" She raised a brow and smiled wider. "That sounds like a good idea, Brett. Just a few of us. Nothing too... mopey?" She leaned in and took her cup of tea to get a drink.

Amanda spoke up as she nodded. "Yeah. The one before was... depressing. I get what a memorial is and all, but we should remember him and be happy, don't ya think?" This girl's smile was hopeful. None of them had been sure of how Ariel would receive the idea.

"Yeah, no. I agree." Ariel assured them and finished off her tea. "But I can't go." Her smile faded to something more sad but she didn't frown. "It's too soon. I really like the idea, though. You guys should do it." Of course it wasn't "too soon", not with what she knew. She was afraid that she might let something slip if the memorial got too emotional, or too drunk.

Her other two friends stayed relatively quiet, frowning and looking away. Brett nodded. "Yeah, we get it. But if ya wanna stop by, it'll be at my place." Amanda nodded in agreement and reached out to touch one of Ariel's hands.

Ariel retracted politely and got up from her seat. "I'll keep that in mind, guys. When are you doing it?" She took her empty cup in her hand as she got ready to leave.

"I was thinkin' tonight around six. Probably go all night." He flashed her a grin. "Just like me." His quip garnered a collective groan from the table.

Ariel chuckled and nodded. "Okay, maybe I'll stop by. Not sure, though." She waved to them and walked out of the cafe after tossing away her cup in the bin. That whole thing was awkward. She shook it off as she began to walk home. A wide grin crossed her face as she thought about Gabriel. The memorial would be good for her friends, but not for her. She walked just about everywhere in the town even though her home was an hour walk from the cafe. As she got closer to her apartment, the sun was going down and it was getting dark rather quickly. Night wasn't something she minded. The town she lived in was relatively safe and she never had a problem walking by herself at night.

Which is why she felt... strange now. She had come to the edge of a park where not many people went, especially not at night. There were hardly any streetlamps to light her way, and it only had become creepy this one time. She felt like someone was watching her but she saw and heard no one at all. In her head she was trying to rationalize what was going on. She didn't know a thing about vampires, but they had to be quiet and well hidden, right? Maybe Gabriel had come back and was just messing with her.

"Gabriel?" She chuckled awkwardly and grimaced. There was a hanging silence that was deafening. The sounds of crickets had died away and any city noise was long gone.

"Gabriel?" A deep voice repeated. It was rich and had a humored tone to it. A man walked into her view, keeping a good distance. He was tall, at least 6'3" and he had long auburn hair pulled back in a neat low tail that went down to his shoulders. His attire was tailored and well made, though the style was strange. It appeared old and unfamiliar and dark. Stranger yet, his skin was flawless and pale and he had deep red eyes that settled onto Ariel with honed intent. He took a step closer to her and grinned.

Whether this guy might have been a vampire or not didn't matter to the young woman. He was a threat and it's not like she had any training in combat and she definitely didn't have any weapons on her. She took a few unsteady steps back, then turned heel and ran. She ran as hard and as fast as she could. She was in good enough shape and had long enough legs that her stride was mildly impressive. To most people.

She suddenly slammed into a solid object that wasn't there before. Right against her was the man who she thought she had left behind. He took ahold of her shoulders and kept her near him. "Gabriel." He repeated again. "You are the girl, then. The one my progeny has been so eager to see. You are greatly hindering my progress with the boy." She leaned into her and his nose nudged against her neck as he inhaled her scent. "Though, it is not difficult to see why. You smell absolutely inviting." Ariel would feel his lips form a smile against her skin. "I'm impressed that he didn't take you the moment he saw you for the first time in his new life."

Ariel felt her vision become blurry for a moment, out of focus. Learning about Gabriel almost caused her to faint before, but now? This man was claiming he was the one who created Gabriel, the new Gabriel. He was impossibly strong with his grip even though it felt like he wasn't trying at all. "I... I..." She stammered out and tried to push him away from her with a grunt. "Let go of me!" She snapped back to reality and began to struggle, though it felt completely in vain.

He scoffed and took a good grip on her thick hair, then jerked her head to the right to give himself plenty of room to caress his lips against her neck. "Mn, wouldn't it be sweet to turn you, as well? Perhaps then you both could be together and be truly powerful." His tongue slipped from his lips just a bit as he ran it against her neck and toward her ear.

"Oh! S-stop that!" She gasped sharply. "A-and what's that supposed to mean?! We're not... he's... let go!" She was flustered and terrified. This jerk was implying that she and Gabriel were more than just friends! ... which would have been nice. She shook her head and used a hand to come around and land a punch on his face.

He made no sound but he did pause. With his hand within her hair, her yanked her head back to force her to look at him. "Or I could slowly drain you and make him watch. Ah, better yet. Force him to help me. Ah, even better! Keep you as a blood doll." His eyes scanned down over her body. "I'm sure you also have other uses, as well."

"Master!" A voice called out and in moments, Gabriel was at his side. "Wait, okay. Stop. I'm sorry. I shouldn't have met with her without your permission. I know I broke the rules." He looked to the man desperately. "Don't hurt her. Please." Gabriel was never one to beg or back down from someone. There was a time before when a drunk guy on the streets was hitting on Ariel and he punched the guy out. Now, though, he was clearly frightened. This man was his "master" and he was acting completely submissive to him.

"Gabriel." The restrained redhead breathed out. Even in her current situation, she was relieved and happy to see him.

"Ah, good boy." Without a thought, the man released Ariel and folded his arms. "She should be killed or turned, Gabriel. Coming out to her like that was a very stupid action." His voice was even and he turned his head to look at the young man beside him.

"I know. I couldn't... I just. I had to see her," He frowned and purposefully looked away from Ariel. "I wanted her to know I wasn't dead."

Ariel looked between them and took a step closer. "Gabriel, I…" Though, she quickly stopped after receiving a sharp look from the larger man.

"You're young. But you should be smarter than that. You put her life in danger and made my life much more difficult. You expect me to hide this, do you not?" What was strange was that his demeanor had softened and he became more… fatherly, in a way. He turned to Gabriel fully and clicked his tongue.

Gabriel didn't respond. It was either a rhetorical question or he had nothing to answer with since his desires were obvious.

The imposing figure turned to me again and held out his hand. "Apologies for the crude encounter, young lady. As enjoyable as I might have found it, I suppose it wasn't fair to be so cruel to you. I was teaching my progeny a lesson in behavior he needs to learn. Though, everything I said was true. The elders would see you killed or turned."

"Ah…" She stammered a little and furrowed her brow.

"Yes, shocking, I'm sure. Do not worry, though. I am Nicoli. Sire to young Gabriel." He motioned to Ariel's best friend.

The young man stepped forward and took her hands in his, subtly moving away from Nicoli. "Sorry, Ariel." He sighed out. "I know this is all fucked up."

Nicoli cleared his throat. "Language, dear boy." He smirked a little. It was difficult to tell if he was serious or not.

Gabriel pursed his lips and rolled his eyes. He stepped closer to Ariel. "I was coming to see you and got…" He wrinkled his nose and huffed like a teenager that was in trouble. "… caught. So all this was my fault." He admitted sourly. "But I want to go talk somewhere. If that's okay." He was asking both of them it seemed.

Ariel broke her awkward silence. "Yeah. I want to. I-"

Nicoli interrupted and chuckled. "Yes, go. For a short while. Make yourself scarce somewhere. I have my hands full hiding your human desires enough as it is." He tapped his fingers on his hips.

Gabriel smiled gratefully and inclined his head. "Thanks." He sighed out, then he took Ariel's hand. "We can go to your apartment, right?"

She nodded slowly. "Yeah." Her eyes wandered to Nicoli who was watching the pair intently.

Without another word, he turned away and began walking in the opposite direction, soon disappearing out of sight.

Ariel led the way to her apartment with Gabriel beside her. They were both silent, allowing their footfalls to do the talking. The void of sound spoke enough for both of them as only the light pat of their feet against the ground made any accent of conversation. Things were... weird. If there was a way to have a casual, lighthearted conversation with your "missing" vampire friend, Ariel hadn't quite nailed down the tact to do so.

Once they arrived, she let him in. Sort of. She walked in and expected him to enter behind her.

He paused.

Ariel looked at him funny. "What…?" He'd been in her apartment dozens of times before.

"Uhm, you know that whole threshold myth with vampires?" He questioned with an awkward intonation. If he could blush, he would be.

There was a hanging silence again. Ariel peered at him with a dubious squint of her eyes. "I have to invite you or you can't come in?" There was something in her voice that was unintelligible. Was she amused by this?

He pursed his lips and folded his arms. "Well, sort of. I could come in. But it'd hurt like Hell and I might pass out." He huffed.

A smile broke onto her lips and she snerked at him. "You're such a cliché." She quipped in a light tone. "Come in then, fangs." She flashed him a grin as if to show her own fangs, which were of course just normal canines.

He rolled his eyes at her. "You're hilarious." He muttered as he walked past her and to her familiar couch, plopping down on it.

"So." Ariel began after shutting the door. "That was your…"

"Master. Sire. New dad." He drawled out dryly.

"And he's…"

"Mad. Or something. Annoyed? It's hard to tell with him." Gabriel waved a hand at her.

She sauntered over to the couch and sat down beside him. "Because?"

Gabriel sighed dramatically and leaned back with his eyes closed. "Because I disobeyed what he said. He told me to not contact anyone from my "old life". It would cause problems. For me, for him."

"How? Well, I guess I kind of get how. But…" Ariel furrowed her brow.

"Baby vampires aren't stable." He admitted gravely. "They've been known to… well, return to their homes and massacre everyone they knew. Some by accident. Some not."

Ariel tensed up. "Oh." She noticeably scooted a bit away from her old friend.

He opened his eyes and sighed. "I won't." He said in a stern voice. "I wouldn't be here if Nicoli thought I would." He paused. "I wouldn't be here if I thought I would."

"Why does he care, anyway? He said something about elders?" She relaxed a little and leaned in toward him.

"Yeah. They're like the politicians of vampires, I guess. They like to be kept underground. Which is probably why no one believes in them." He wrinkled his nose. "In us. So when someone fucks it up-" He pointed to himself. "They get a little antsy."

"Then why does Nicoli let you? He obviously wasn't happy about it."

"He's... different. It's been a long time since he's been human. But he remembers." Gabriel frowned softly. "He's called a human sympathizer. Which isn't really a nice thing with vampires. We're supposed to be different, better. Humans are food and playthings." He tilted her head over to her. "I don't know what I'm gonna be like as more time passes. Maybe having Nicoli as a sire'll keep me from becoming a total monster."

"Ah." Ariel breathed out and took his hand. "You'll always be you, Gabriel."

He scoffed, glancing down toward their joined hands. "No." His voice was soft, dreary. "I'm not. I'll never be me again. I don't know how to explain it. It's like… being possessed. Forever. I can still see, hear, feel, think. But my mind… it's different." He furrowed his brow. "I think and feel things I've never thought of before. But now it's second nature."

His friend was at a loss for words as he spoke. She couldn't possibly understand and there was no use in trying. She knew that. "Gabriel." She leaned in and wrapped her arms around him in a gentle embrace.

His hand slid up her back and tangled within her soft hair. "Ariel." He murmured against her hair as he held her close. "There's something else about me you should know." He kept her close and didn't move.

"Something else?" She remarked, almost bewildered that there could possibly be anything that mattered more than being a vampire.

"What I am... "vampire" doesn't cover it. Not like we knew it in stories. There are different types of vampires. Like, everyone has a different power. Sometimes a different hunger, too." He sighed and groaned quietly. He didn't want to tell her any of this.

Even at his pause, she didn't say anything. He would get to his point in due time. It was obviously difficult for him.

"I can sedate people." He picked over the words carefully and she could feel his lips purse a bit against her head. "Uhm, you know what incubi are?" The words were definitely forced.

Ariel's cheeks flushed and she cleared her throat. Her quickened heartbeat was unmistakable to her friend's keen senses. "Yeah."

"I can make people... er, aroused. But when I... ya know, I'd siphon their energy. It'd kill someone over time. Like if it was every single day. It would make me feel better. Like blood. But I need that, too." His voice soured. It was irritating that he required two sources of energy. The balance didn't seem fair. Other vampires could do things like read minds, turn into things, and even fly. While being able to seduce someone might be enjoyable, the addition of needing the talent to siphon the required energy seemed like a bum deal.

She slowly nodded. It was easy enough to understand. "You talk like you've never done it."

"I haven't." He admitted with a matter-of-fact cadence.

Ariel lifted her head and looked at him incredulously.

He rolled his eyes. "I haven't as a vampire." He scoffed at her. "I didn't mean I never have."

She grinned at him. "Okay, okay. Just making sure." Her expression faded into a more solemn mask. "Will you ever…?"

He shrugged. "It's weird. I'll have to at some point probably. But I've never really been into random sex. Maybe being like this long enough will change that."

"I see." Ariel bit her bottom lip and furrowed her brow. She wasn't sure what to say to that. She felt… jealous. But jealous of what? There was no one to be envious of. It was the idea that flustered her so much.

"Something wrong?" He tilted his head as he looked at her with a curious, if not smug, expression.

She shrugged and shook her head. "No. Why?"

There was a hanging silence and then Gabriel's hand was touching against his friend's cheek very lightly to turn her head to look at him. "It's hard to hide from me now that I'm like this. I had a feeling before, but… "

Ariel furrowed her brow. "Huh?"

"The way your heart's beating. Your scent. Your breathing." He leaned in closer, causing her back to press against the arm of the couch. "You have feelings for me, don't you? I wasn't sure before. You know... before all this. I didn't want to ask and make things weird."

"And this isn't weird?" She mused with a nervous and awkward tone.

He shrugged. "Weird is relevant now." He moved forward again and dipped his head so that his lips were at her neck. "We're idiots. I've wanted you for a long time, Ariel. Now that I know for sure..." His right hand to her left and he intertwined their fingers. It was a sweet gesture but his strength was also holding her down against the couch. His lips caressed against her neck and soon he began to kiss over her nape and down to her collarbone and then to her ear. "Do you have anything to do tomorrow?" He murmured near her ear.

At first, she was frozen. Arousal and a mild amount of fear and uncertainty caused her to mold to his actions. When he asked her that question, she came back to the moment and blinked a few times. She hadn't even noticed that her breathing picked up and she was even throbbing softly between her legs. "Uh, no... why?"

"I can't control my hunger yet." He hedged. "But I want you. And if we do anything, you'll be really tired afterward. Maybe need a day to recover." Even so, he started to nip over her neck and his freehand slid up her shirt and under her bra. Without any hesitation, he cupped and lightly squeezed her bare breast.

She gasped sharply and bit her bottom lip. He had never been a forward person. Maybe he was right. He wasn't completely himself now. Or parts of him he already had were unlocked to run rampant in his new being. All that being said, she couldn't say she didn't like it. "You mean what we were just talking about? No biting, right?" She grimaced at the thought, but she was also shamefully curious.

There was a pause and Gabriel leaned back to look into her eyes. "More than likely." He had a lopsided grin but he wasn't completely joking, either. "It doesn't hurt." He insisted and shuddered a little. Now he was thinking about that, too. Sating two of his hungers with the girl he wanted for so long. That was a heavy temptation.

Ariel pursed her lips, her gaze hesitant. "Can I trust you?"

Another pause. "I hope so." At the very least, he was honest. He wasn't sure what his new self would do once in the moment. What he did know was that he'd hate himself if he really hurt her. And his sire would come down on him like a ton of bricks. A lot of "I told you so" and likely some physical and mental lashings.

His answer didn't make his friend, his more than a friend, very calm. "Ah…" She bit her bottom lip and looked away. "I think I can." She finally breathed out, throwing caution to the wind.

That was all the reassurance that the newborn vampire needed. He leaned in and kissed her fervently, his hand still pushing her against the arm of the couch. He quickly deepened the kiss and felt his own tongue against hers. She was amazingly warm in comparison to him, and the feeling of life invigorated him with a profound need and desire. Before he knew it, his hand went from beneath her shirt and jerked on it. If he had more human like strength, it would have jerked her body and possibly left fabric burns over her neck and shoulders. His tenacity was well centered and precise, though. Without hardly a jolt of her body, the shirt tore in half and was left in tatters around her frame. He was more careful with her bra and simply unclasped the back of it and tossed it off of her arms. Now that her top was bare to him, he groaned softly. His lips trailed from her neck and down to her breasts, kissing gently around her nipples without quite touching them.

Ariel bit her bottom lip and arched her back. "They're holding a memorial for you." She murmured absently. Her voice was soft and it was undoubtedly an afterthought to the situation. It was something she meant to tell him before the current situation unfolded. Her cheeks were flushed light red to match how warm she felt. Her soft, pink nipples were becoming stiff just from him being near them.

He glanced up for a moment, appearing thoughtful. "Oh?" His lips returned to her breasts, kissing and caressing over each one as his hands held onto her hips. They were rather eager themselves but behaved for the time being.

She tried to relax a little and simply enjoy the moment. Even if this was something she wanted, it didn't stop her from being a bit timid. It all felt so surreal. It really was. "Uh...huh." She breathed out and closed her eyes. "Just some friends. I didn't go." She paused and smiled wryly. "Obviously."

"Good." His voice was a subdued growl. He couldn't hold himself back any longer. Teasing her was fun, but he needed more. His lips closed around one of her nipples and he began to suck on it gently, sliding his tongue against every part of it.

She gasped sharply and arched her back. "Mn!" A gentle moan escaped her pouted lips.

"This is a better memorial, don't ya think?" He stopped to murmur that, giving short sucks and kisses to that nipple before moving to the other. "You're so aroused." A chuckle touched his voice. He must have been able to pick up her scent between her legs.

"Ah! Gabriel!" She protested with a self-conscious whine. She could figure out what he was meaning, given how he nonchalantly listed off how he knew she desired him.

"Mn? Oh, don't be so shy about it. It's taking everything I have in me to not rip your pants off and fuck you until you scream." He cooed to her with an overpowering amount of lust in his voice.

"... mmf." She huffed faintly. She couldn't really argue with that. She was almost tempted to tell him to stop holding himself back. But they had time. Ariel shifted a bit on the couch, sliding her right leg off as her left raised up a little against the back of the couch. It allowed Gabriel to slid between them more as he went back to paying attention to her breasts.

His hands slipped up from her hips to grasp both of them at the sides, squeezing them inward. It allowed him to slide his tongue over both of her nipplesand suck on them with lewd pops when he'd release them. "Mm..." He moaned against her then continued to suck and tug on them to get them nice and stiff. After a few more moments, he released her breasts and let them bounce. "Shit, Ariel." He sighed out and sat up between her legs while on his knees. It became evident what his curse was about when he tugged down his pants and underwear and his sizeable cock sprung free from its confines. He was fully hard. A good guess would place him at about eight inches and one and half around.

Ariel had no idea her best friend was so... gifted. That seemed like the appropriate wording in her clouded mind. She sat up a bit then reached out and brushed her fingers against him. "Wow." She breathed out with an awkward titter of a laugh, a lopsided smile on her soft lips. Her hand gradually wrapped around him and she began to feel over every curve and detail. As she did, she felt a gush of arousal from her slit between her legs, effectively ruining her panties.

The deepening of her need wasn't lost on Gabriel. He grinned at her and leaned in, causing his length to slip away just a bit. "I'm glad my cock gets such a reaction out of you, Ari." He used an old nickname of hers that he would say when teasing her or being playful. His hand slipped between her legs and into her pants and panties. He wasn't going to tease her this time as he had been. His deft fingers slid between the lips of her pussy and stroked over them and against her interest. They easily slid because of how wet she was and he almost lost his finger inside of her if he didn't stop himself. He felt around it and sighed out. "You feel so tight already. The neighbors are gonna complain soon." He flashed her a toothy grin.

She gasped sharply and shuddered, lifting her left leg all the way over the couch so that she was spread lewdly in front of him. Her hand was forced to let go of his throbbing manhood and she became a bit selfish now that he was touching her. "I... I..." She stammered and groaned, whimpering in need. "Stop teasing me, Gabriel!"

He quirked a brow and smirked at her. "Teasing? I'm touching your pussy, Ari. Or do you want more?" His middle finger moved up and started rubbing at her clit, forcing the hood of it back to toy with it directly. He achieved the desired reaction as Ariel bucked against his hand and cried out a bit loudly. She was an absolute mess, her couch damp along with her slit and her thighs and now Gabriel's hand. He flawlessly switched his middle digit with his thumb so that the longer finger would easily slip into her wanting entrance as his thumbed toyed with her little button. Even though she was tight, the amount of sticky arousal she produced was more than enough to allow him to slip in and be hugged by her inner walls.

"Nn! Gabriel!" Her hips lifted up a little and she moved closer to him by a small fraction. Her hands went down to her pants and she hooked her thumbs within them and her panties, jerking them down until they hung limply around her right ankle. "I can't take it. I need you." She had never felt like this before. her lust was staggering and she felt like she was so hot she could faint.

He leaned into her, causing his cock to press close, rubbing against her thigh. He slowly removed his finger and lowered his head to kiss her neck. "Shit." He sighed out with a sardonic chuckle. "I can't control my influence on you." He admitted. This was the key to her intense need for him, it seemed. "Just my own need and presence is making you into a slut." He kissed to her ear and gave it a small nip. "I like it." Just a moment later, he pushed his hips forward and made no ceremony about stuffing his entire length inside of her. He cried out shortly and began to take precise, terse thrusts into her. He pulled out half way then met with the back of her walls with a quick, deep thrust. "Let me feed on you, Ariel. From... ah, from now on. Please. I don't want any other woman. You feel so perfect!" He slid his hand to the back of her hair and took a handful of her striking locks. He used his grip to tilt her head back and to the side to really get at her neck with rough nips and firm kisses. All the while, his hips moved against her in a steady rhythm and untiring.

Her head was swimming. She heard everything he said but she didn't have the capacity to really process it and come up with a concise, well thought reply. This was something she should be thinking about. It wasn't just some careless decision. It didn't seem to matter, though. Her body reacted perfectly to his. Every inch of her was on fire. As he pushed into her over and over, small squirts of her arousal painted the couch beneath them in such a copious amount she didn't think she'd be able to achieve something like this ever again without him. Without their chest pressing together, her breasts bounced heavily with each thrust and gave the man atop her an incredible view. "Mn! Yes... I... I will." She panted out, condemning herself to being the food and plaything of her vampiric best friend. In the moment, it felt more like a reward than a sentence. Ariel's hands lifted and she used them to roughly grab her breasts and grope them, tugging on her sensitive nipples and twisting them gently between her fingers.

"Cum for me. I need it." He growled out, quickening his thrusts and positioning his hips to hit her exactly where she needed it. His incubi like instincts were kicking in and guiding him, subconsciously knowing how to pleasure Ariel, and pleasure her specifically. He jerked her head back, each touch and movement of his becoming more harsh and uncaring of his partner's comfort. His lips pressed against her neck and before he could hold himself back, pointed fangs sunk into her flesh. He let out a loud, muffled moan against her as a spray of crimson entered his mouth. He wasn't a very clean eater in the throes of passion, because plenty of her lifesource dripped down her neck from between his lips. It stained her skin and over her breasts as well.

Her eyes widened in shock, confusion, pleasure. No pain, just as he said. It should have hurt by all rights. His teeth were digging into her neck and all she felt was a surge of arousal squirting against his cock that was buried deeply inside of her. She reached up and took a handful of his short hair, pressing him closer against her as her hips writhed and undulated beneath him. It took seconds more for her to reach her peak and cry out loudly. Her body went stiff and she lifted her right leg to wrap around his waist. Her hips bucked against his as she climaxed, riding it out on his thick, throbbing cock. She would definitely need to get her couch cleaned soon. "Gabriel!" She gasped breathlessly, whimpering and whining softly as her body still throbbed and yearned for more.

He released her neck and lifted up quickly. "Fuck." He groaned out in pleasure and remorse combined. He hadn't meant to bite her. That along with his incubus like power would leave her drained for days possibly. Even though she protested with quiet whines, he slid back until his length slipped from her grasping hole. He licked his lips and shuddered. "You look... so sexy like that." His voice was husky with a hint of a growl behind it. As he looked over her body, he shuddered. There was a splash of blood in her neck with trickles of it over her heaving breasts. She was a bit more pale because of the loss of the crimson liquid as well as the energy he took when she orgasmed. Her hair was a well placed mess, as if positioned and styled on purpose to look absolutely ravaged by the man above her. Not only that, but a glance between them would prove that her tight entrance had stretched a bit to perfectly accommodate his length and no one else's. Everything about her current state screamed that she belonged to him. And vampires were really, really into possession.

Ariel whimpered softly and arched her back a bit as she squirmed faintly. "Gabriel..." Her voice was a distant sigh. Her leg slipped from his waist and landed back onto the floor where it began as her other leg started to slide back down from the back of the couch. She was in a state of euphoria, a bit dizzy but feeling pleasure throughout her entire body. In a way, it felt deadly. It was something she couldn't have too often, too intense for her body to handle on a consistent basis. That didn't stop her from wanting it, craving it.

Gabriel could somewhat tell what was going on in her head. It was something his master warned him about. But he felt sort of proud for making Ariel feel such intense pleasure. After this, he would have to be careful. Though, he knew she would be addicted to him and to the sensations. He almost felt guilty about it, but that was overshadowed by his cock that was still throbbing and ready for more. He smiled to her and easily maneuvered her body that that she was on her stomach on the couch still. "Work with me, Ari." He chided her as she zoned out in blissful ignorance.

When she heard him speak, though, she perked up and came back to the real world. "Ah..." When she realized what he was doing, she made her body more rigid but also pliable. She placed her left knee against the couch while settling the sole of her right foot onto the floor. "I feel so empty." She whined at him, using her fingers to spread her lips enticingly.

"Mn, yes. Because you need me." He responded with smug causality. He rested a hand on her hips while the other took his slick cock and he rubbed it teasingly against her entrance. "Try not to orgasm too much. Like I said, I can't control my power very well. You might pass out." He was being teasing but also serious. It was a very real possibility that she might lose consciousness if she "allowed" him to take too much of her energy, not to mention the loss of blood just moments ago.

"Funny..." She huffed in mild annoyance, particularly because she felt like she'd collapse if she didn't have him inside of her soon. She kept her hips lifted up high at the perfect height for him to push into her and move with ease. "You know... I won't cum so much if you did. I want to feel it. I-I need to feel it." She groaned with lust.

"I know." He said with a self-satisfied tone. It was intoxicating, the power he had over her right now. He shouldn't have enjoyed it, so much, but he did. His best friend was under his influence, but she was doing so under her own consent. He explained the best he could what could happen and she still wanted him. He bit his bottom lip gently and pushed forward, now slowly feeding her cunt his cock. "Ah... shit." He groaned, doing well to hold himself back. Eventually he did end up buried inside of her, allowing her to feel every inch of his throbbing length. He leaned over her and reached beneath her to grasp her breasts.

"You're teasing me again..." She sighed out within a gentle moan. Her nipples were still hard and aching to be toyed with. Their session was messy enough that their combined arousal, her wetness and his pre-cum, was slowly dripping onto the couch from the seal his cock made within her pussy. Any movement they made allowed a bit to escape and dampen her couch. She wiggled her hips, grinding back against him.

"Only a little." He insisted, sounding more like his old, playful self. He used the leverage he had on her breasts to keep himself against her. It didn't allow him to pull out fully as he had before, so he took shorter, staccato thrusts against her. His fingers toyed with her nipples now, tugging at them firmly and rolling them around between his fingers. "I've never felt this good, Ari..." He panted out against her ear. "Do you want me to cum?"

Her back was arched in a way that suggested she was very limber and flexible, and it allowed him to be bent over her as he was. She was moaning heavily, not quite as loudly as before until he began to pick up the pace, hammering against her most sensitive parts. "Yes! Oh fuck, hurry... I'm going to cum soon!" She pleaded with him. She desperately wanted to climax again, but she was a little hesitant because of what he said. Not only that, but she deeply desired his own orgasm and the feeling of his seed filling her. It was something she'd been longing for for years now.

He wanted to feel her climax again, too. Even in his lust driven state, he had enough sense to give her mercy. Gabriel wasn't sure how another orgasm would affect her, so she quickened his pace. He grunted with each thrust, feeling her walls rub and tug against him as if trying to milk his cock. "Fuck..." He panted out, soon pressing fully within her as he released his cum. He stayed planted deep inside of her as he unloaded himself in quick spurts. He then pulled his hips back and a few strands of his thick cum landed on the swollen lips of her abused pussy. He fell back onto the couch and panted. "Ariel..." He placed his arm over his forehead, his hips still idly rocking a bit as his body squirmed.

The exhausted woman slumped down onto her couch, causing her cum covered pussy to squish against the fabric. She couldn't care at the moment, though. She was lightheaded and groggy, stuck in a state of heightened bliss. "Amazing..." She managed to breathe out.

"Dammit." Gabriel growled suddenly. He looked down to his cock which was still stiff and throbbing wildly. He knew he couldn't keep fucking her, though. Not without some sort of risk involved.

When she heard him utter the curse, she willed herself to sit up and adjust so she was facing him. "Huh?" She furrowed her brow, a dreamy expression still on her face.

"I'm still hard." He muttered, as if it was a bad thing. It wouldn't have been if he was anyone -anything- else.

It took her a few moments, but Ariel soon realized why that was a "bad" thing. "Oh. Well…" She moved up toward him and bent over between his legs as she faced him. "You don't have to fuck me to cum." Her voice was sweet and it matched her loving smile despite the completely lewd situation.

He got the gist of what she was implying. He smirked to her and sat up, leaning back against the arm of the couch. "I can't believe I've made you this cock hungry."

She shrugged helplessly. "You monster." A tease, of course. Her right hand cupped his heavy balls, still full of more seed he needed to release. As she gently caressed them, her head came forward and her tongue ran up from the base of his length to the very tip. The entire flat of her tongue rolled over him and she swallowed any cum that she gathered.

He tensed up for a moment and groaned in pleasure. "Can you taste yourself on me?"

"Mn…" She hummed out. It caused soft, pleasant vibrations on him. The little technique granted her a bead of his precum mixed with some of the seed he had expelled earlier. She licked that off and began to suckle on the head of his cock, slowly taking more of his thick length.

"Yes… ah. I didn't know you were so good at sucking cock, Ari." A grin tugged at his lips. Then he placed his hand on top of her head and stroked her hair gently. "But I think you can take more." His soft touch turned rough when he used his grip to push her down onto his cock entirely. He pressed back against her throat and made a small bulge in it because of how much he stuffed into her mouth. "Oh!" He groaned out and began to buck his hips to start fucking her mouth. "Sorry! It feels so fucking good, Ari!" His voice was husky again and he didn't slow down at all.

Her eyes went wide when she was suddenly full of his length, feeling it pound against her throat and making her gag. It was too much and made the moment even more messy as he drug out his saliva along with his precum. Her hands went to his thighs to steady herself as they trembled and her fingers pressed firmly against his skin. Her sore pussy was throbbing deeply and his cum and her new arousal were dripping out steadily. She had no idea her body would react in such a way from being face-fucked by her best friend. Gabriel likely had no idea either. She soon relaxed and didn't struggle so much as he used her as his own personal fucktoy to get to his next orgasm, She wasn't even being touched, but she moaned in pleasure.

Gabriel gave her opportunities to catch her breath but did so only momentarily until he was filling her mouth again. He was lying back over the arm of the couch as he really raised his hips up and thrust against her in a manner most men would only do if they were inside of a woman's pussy. He seemed to be getting even more thick as he approached his second orgasm. "Amazing! Ariel!"

Feeling him engorge more like he was was too much for the young woman. She tensed up and cried out, muffled by his cock. Her pussy twitched a little as she came suddenly and squirted her arousal onto the couch for a good three seconds before it subsided. This was something that only Gabriel would be able to achieve for sure. His power that incited such lust within her human mind allowed her to do thing she never thought possible. It would be difficult keeping herself away from him on a daily basis.

Gabriel wasn't expecting his partner to climax. The feeling of energy that it gave him was overpowering and forced his hand. He came hard and filled her mouth, forcing most of it down her throat. As she gagged and coughed, he pulled back and emptied the rest of his hot load onto her face and her breasts. He grinned and released his grip on her head as he fell back. "Shit, Ariel. Sorry…. I didn't know that you'd-" He stopped and looked down at her. "Ariel?" He blinked a few times.

The girl had promptly passed out, still breathing of course, and was halfway off the couch. She was covered in cum, blood, and saliva. All evidence of the moment they just shared.

He reached down and nudged her lightly. "Uh…"

She didn't react to his touch at all. She had been forced into a deep slumber to try and recover his physical and mental resources. He had taken too much from her.

"Crap." Gabriel sighed out. He furrowed his brow. He leaned forward and got her back onto the couch so that she was lying on her back. He looked her over and bit his lip. They were polar opposites at that very moment. She was in a supernatural slumber while he felt perfectly energized and ready to conquer the world. Well, conquer the world excluding his master. Shit, he was going to be pissed. Or amused. Probably both. He moved off of the couch and looked down at her. Nope, she was still hot. "Im a real piece of shit." He sighed out and rubbed the back of his head. He knew she'd be okay. But she might not wake up for another entire day. He couldn't just leave her there, much less covered in such a mess.

The vampire, who was a mess himself, took out his phone and hit a contact in his "favorites". "Master?" He uttered. After a few seconds of the man on the other end speaking, Gabriel sighed. "... yeah, I did. Can I stay here with her until she wakes up?" Another bout of silence from the baby vampire. "Yeah, I figured." He sighed out deeply. "I'll take my punishment after I get back. ... thanks." He pressed the red phone icon to end the call and looked over to Ariel. "Yay, a slumber party." He mused bitterly. At least his master had allowed him to stay.